SILVERFIN
THE GRAPHIC NOVEL

CHARLIE HIGSON
&
KEV WALKER

Disney · HYPERION BOOKS

NEW YORK

PART ONE

ETON

PART TWO

SCOTLAND

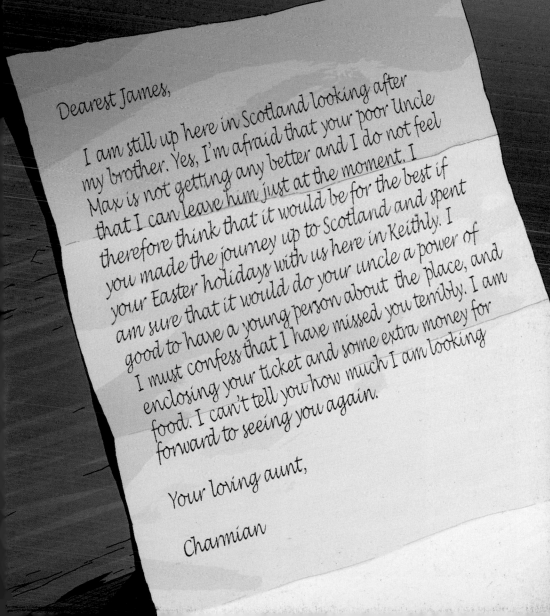

Dearest James,

I am still up here in Scotland looking after my brother. Yes, I'm afraid that your poor Uncle Max is not getting any better and I do not feel that I can leave him just at the moment. I therefore think that it would be for the best if you made the journey up to Scotland and spent your Easter holidays with us here in Keithly. I am sure that it would do your uncle a power of good to have a young person about the place, and I must confess that I have missed you terribly. I am enclosing your ticket and some extra money for food. I can't tell you how much I am looking forward to seeing you again.

Your loving aunt,

Charmian

Dearest Mother,
I know I have never written to you before, but lately I have been thinking about you a great deal . . .

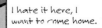

I hate it here, I want to come home.

PART THREE

SILVERFIN

Adapted from the novel *SilverFin: A James Bond Adventure* by Charlie Higson
Adapted by Kev Walker
Scripted by Charlie Higson and Kev Walker
Lettering by Annie Parkhouse

Published by Disney • Hyperion Books, an imprint of Disney Book Group. No part of this
book may be reproduced or transmitted in any form or by any means, electronic or
mechanical, including photocopying, recording, or by any information storage and
retrieval system, without written permission from the publisher.

For information address Disney • Hyperion Books,
114 Fifth Avenue, New York, New York 10011-5690.

First American edition, 2010
10 9 8 7 6 5 4 3 2 1
Printed in Singapore

Library of Congress Cataloging-in-Publication Data on file.
ISBN 978-1-4231-3022-2 (hardcover)
ISBN 978-1-4231-3023-9 (paperback)

Visit www.youngbond.com and www.hyperionbooksforchildren.com